PEACE IN PARADISE

Songs For A City In The Sun

By

George O. Obikoya

Book 1

Once upon a time, there was a city in the sun, a place of immense wealth where everyone was happy, enjoyed life, never had to starve, a city where people lived long and healthy lives, wherein life was blissful, peace prevailed over war in ages past, long before the paradise it became, when life became worth living again, and even the sun smiled again, verily unveiling the atavistic joy it missed, for long, as the city did not cry again, as it flourished again, its music its art its culture its science all bloomed, again, renewed in all ways was the city in the sun, the city that became the envy of the realms, the place to be, venturing free in the realms perfection everywhere displayed, in sundry manners yea, as in the city in the sun, a place where auric-laden cobblestones carpeted streets and alleys, where drumbeats of cosmic rains caressed the tympani with sweet melodies of atmospheric songs, that celestial choirs dispensed.

This pleasant city in the sun was free of stress and pain, agony there did not exist, there were no fights nor were there conflicts anywhere in it, love, peace and harmony were what therein prevailed, a city where everyone cared about one another, one in which people joined hands to improve their lots, to enhance their abilities to improve the city, their reality, happy they all were to admit they forged in forges from a lower to a higher even more perfect form, a version they all intended to keep working on to improve yea its state, to make the city what they truly wanted it to be at any point in time: a more perfect version than heretofore more perfect than before the one that was also more perfect than the one before its form before, ad infinitum going back, to make the city increasingly much better than before, ad infinitum going ahead, the goal, qualitative improvements everywhere they looked, therein.

The peoples of the city in the sun were cognizant of the days of yore, when war was second-nature to the ones before, the ones who fought over almost everything ranging from a piece of real estate in some remote location in a arid land, or in the ocean deep, to a bowl of rice, ostensibly treasure-hunting for a city lost in millennials gone, or simply feeling strong spoiling for a fight: O yes, they were, and they were determined not to create any such reality let alone embrace or nurture it in a city of the sun, again, but to stay the course, forward ever move their precious world, so, they all worked very hard to ensure that nothing came in the way of achieving their stated aim: nothing but their 'collective unconscious,' in Jungian parlance forward drove their cause, they were resolute and strong, morally strong, they brooked no front-door meta-narratives nor did they, any, that might attempt to sneak in through the back door.

They remembered what it took to, literally, peel these parasitic narratives off their skins to get to where they were, they did not forget what they went through to shear the processes and forces behind these narratives off their pates, to be free of their power, perniciousness and seemingly unstoppable control over what they thought, even what and how they felt; they still remembered the many faces of inequality that grand narratives perpetuated, the bigotry, divisions in society based on presumed racial and gender differences, and the class differences that economic disparities generated, they did not forget about the eugenics movement and that they must justify their existence every five years, they also remembered historicism, that circumstances and implicit processes that were beyond their control determined or affected goings on their world: verily, they took these things to heart, yes.

They knew they had to revisit the frameworks on which they pivoted their knowledge of the world and,
embrace necessary paradigmatic shifts to forge ahead with making the city better,
increasingly better and more perfect for the good of all, and they knew it was not easy to
shake off dated notions to embrace new ones: not at all, they all went through hell persuading their
folks to rid themselves of the cryptic machinations in void of the implicit processes and
circumstances beyond their control, the forces they variously termed entities, or archons,
'spiritual wickedness in high places,' viruses, parasites, ghosts, and Satan, yes, Satan
whose iterations as Satan, the key angel, along with Michael and Gabriel, they traced, from
the angel God used to send to test the faith of people, such as in the case of Job of Uz, or
to punish them, onto a new Satan, one emergent into a new entity, to fight God.

They talked about Satan, and they modified their views about the entity, including among
others, preferring to term the notion of God doing both good things and evil things as 'picture thinking'
a mythological metaphor of liberal theology to describe an entity
operating outside the human body which, however, it could influence, invade, also
affect, pretty much like historicism said about the implicit processes, forces that
were beyond human control: they tried to understand how this erstwhile emissary of God turned
an adversary of God, out to wage war against God and cause pain in the world, operated
in a city of the sun that they were trying to figure how to make a more perfect place, dead
set not to lose their gains as they continued to navigate the perilous terrains along the
way, set to probe riddles such as the baring of Enoch, Ezekiel and Elijah to 'beings.'

It was tough for them to even contemplate letting go their accomplishments not to mention being
complacent about the future of their world: they realized the need for them to value both, and
how not doing so was tantamount to giving up on their city and, in effect, on themselves
for, after all they had been through, and were continuously going through, that they all created,
incrementally, their shared reality was no longer in doubt, as was not, that the notion
of artificial intelligence was bogus: they knew that intelligence was an aspect of
consciousness, that sired it in reality they shared, with 'hidden hands' controlling matters behind
the scenes as they had done since immemorial days, they knew that the little agency they had
to steer their reality was what helped free them from the fangs of their overlords, remade their world,
despite the intrigues of coalitions jostling to evince the consciousness of their shared truth, O yea.

There was no gainsaying they were always under threat: they knew it, pretty much as they knew that the
1919 Versailles Treaty portended a future war, and that some 'machine' would, in time, pass
the Turin's test, that the progression toward singularity would not only be defined by
secularity but also by spirituality, and they harked back to a trial in
1925, the Scopes Money Trial, they knew they were under threat of an alliance of
players or perhaps, ghosts, embroiled verily in politico-economic transactions and
their populist mates, to attain economic gains via populist pains, O well, masquerading
as gains, for who had the bowl of rice peoples asked, and were threatening, O yes, to have it again?
The peoples' eyes were at last opened to the chicanery of ghosts, and 'folks,' added to the mix,
suggestive of mystical or spiritual forces at play: they thought about archons, O yea.

They thought about who or what taught the Dogons about Sirius prior, it seemed, to teaching the

'West' they thought about a lot of things, and they were always under threat, O yes, under threat of the
resurgence of fanaticism in the city, with folks beholden to emissaries of
whoever or whatever was operating in the shadows to impose their agenda on
inhabitants of the city via grand narratives that purportedly comprised the truth, a claim they
long ago realized was an inversion of the truth meant to confuse everyone, pretty much
like the debate over socialism notwithstanding the hidden hands being prickly about being
exposed, and doing everything to dumb down the folks, pay them off, the universal basic thing,
sorry, income thing, and entertain them, robots' jobs, tell us about it, they said, define it, what?
socialism! The folks meant business; keen to reach higher not lower realms, more perfect, ever.

Mistakes were made over the years, they liked to say, perhaps to concede that imperfect they also
were, an admission that they figured would help them to always be vigilant and not allow their
errors to drag them down a rabbit hole, errors made by their predecessors, such as allowing
the debt-to-GDP ratio to go past ninety percent, which in effect, bankrupted the
city, anathema they all dreaded, a situation they were all determined to prevent from
ever happening again, as they resolved to not anything nor anyone, no matter how
pernicious, how miasmic, how malicious, or how dangerous, destroy their precious world, one they
fought so hard to mould into what it was for them, a city in the sun they paid so much in gore
sweat and tears yes to create, to ever more perfect make, wherein ascension was on every lip,
as indeed, it was in every heart, a state of peace wherein they trysted with folks in the realms, sought.

Book 2

Yes, they sought to venture in the realms in a continuum of consciousness they all worked hard to attain, they commerced with others in the realms with goodwill in their hearts for all, not unwary they were constantly under threat, if even, everyone joked and laughed with them, verily foes they knew they had walking among them in the city yea, in the city of the sun where peace and love reigned: they knew they had to keep working hard to ward off their enemies within and outside the city, and they were determined so to do, they were aware of the pervasiveness of the hidden hands, for example, in the affairs of the world, over the ages, how they set up institutions, policies and processes in every sphere of life to keep people in line, and to keep people silent and compliant, or face lousy references from their current bosses, or from their bosses wherever they had worked, tactics they knew caused inequality, that created divisions, chaos.

It was tough removing themselves from shackles that held them down for so very long, shackles that tied them to grand narratives that reinforced their statuses as slaves, effectively, persons that had to obey the commands of a 'group think' leader no matter how unreasonable they were, for example, an order not to wear face masks, and not to follow the guidelines recommended by experts, aimed at preventing the spread of a deadly virus in a pandemic: they did not at all lose sight of their struggles to free themselves from whoever or whatever was 'dishing out' and 'obeying' the orders giving what their studies informed them about the amalgams that they were, that they were composites of consciousnesses jostling for manifestations as realities they shared; they remembered their struggles to not let imposed grand narratives lead them into hell, the abyss, their quest to break free of mind-control hidden hands perpetuated everywhere in their world.

Their bid to break free of the hidden hands did not take long after they all chose to use the little agency they had to reconfigure their consciousnesses in what yea seemed to be a David and Goliath situation, a point at which their erstwhile overlords overstepped their bounds and yes, lost control, even if momentarily, but with quite humongous consequences for the mammoth sway they held over every other consciousness, big or small: verily, it was a huge paradigmatic shift that unity yes, amongst hitherto divided peoples in their world assured, unity that enabled the peoples to choose, at last, on their own, unfettered by the purveyors of the grand narratives that held the peoples back for so very long, that ingrained in their collective psyche the notion that they were cybernetic beings, you know, some biotic cum coded entities, you know, some sort of hybrid, cyborg, you know, some kind of singularity.

Yes, they broke free of the grand narratives of science, saw through the notions of technological singularity as opposed to spiritual singularity, O yes, the usual dichotomizations, black and white, male and female, rich and poor, they saw the gist of the debt-to -GDP ratio being past a hundred percent, and the unceasing rise of inherited wealth, yes, the inevitable squeeze and shakeout of the 'nouveau riche:' the whole shebang, yes, all of which unity dissolved, revealed to the peoples, secrets of the magi as some preferred to say, the underbelly of the snake exposed; so, they found out that they were all indeed reality-creating amalgams and nothing else, and that they could, indeed chart their path to wherever they wished, which they did, the path toward creating a more perfect reality, chose, not one that would have led them down the path of the fangs of an ouroboros recycled in a viper, and snaked.

They knew all along they had to be free of the machinations of the hidden hands, the forces
that ever manipulated their realities in a voided spacetime they seemed able not
to flee, they knew, based on what they gleaned in their study that in an accretion of realities,
including their physical selves and all that were mattered in their world, their consciousnesses indeed,
manifested over time: they knew their presumed fate, one controlled by hidden processes beyond
their control, inherent in their world, via realities, which their consciousnesses begot, O yes,
a situation which, however, they tired not, seeking to change, which they finally did, freed themselves
of all manner of grand narratives that dumbed them down, led them down the path of negativity,
and of destruction debasing wearing a face mask to prevent the spread of a virus yes in
a pandemic, for instance, they chose the path of positivity, which took them to where they were.

It was terrific, as anyone would imagine, that they finally wrenched control of their world
from their erstwhile overlords forming their own, clearly, more potent alliances uniting their
once divided peoples after all, peoples once divided by inequality that many
strategies and tactics instituted and perpetrated by hidden hands perpetuated
in their voided spacetime O yes, their realities predominant patently malevolent
consciousnesses begot, but they knew they were constantly under threat, and were vigilant lest they
lost focus and let the hidden hands gain the upper hand once again, the last thing they would ever
wish for in a world that they were in control, so, they all kept a close eye on the 'divide-and-rule'
'experts' in their midst, the propounders and sponsors of grand narratives that created a state of
turmoil, with the split made between 'natural' and 'artificial' intelligences for instance.

The peoples asked what intelligence meant to the splitters, the dichotomizers: perhaps it was
passing the Turin test, or it was the speed of creating algorithms, or of processing
data of all sorts, including Freudian slips, you know, the 'herd mentality' thing the peoples
also heard, 'mistook' for herd immunity, or if it meant being sapient plus sentient and,
sophisticatedly too, or whatever! They rejected being considered a herd goaded like
goats, immersed in lixiviating credos and ideologies led with chains like slaves; they all
concluded that, certainly, intelligence, to the splitters did not mean intellectually
yoking with ane, a state the peoples considered intellectually and spiritually,
interchangeable as in the interchangeability of both in the path yes to
ascension, which the peoples, as one, chose and, as one were bent on treading for evermore, unfazed.

'Vigilance ever' was their motto 'forward ever, never backward' was their mantra, and forging
a more perfect union was their stated goal, to the chagrin of the splitters walking in their
midst, working to tear apart a city in the sun, they were well aware of the threat that entrenched
narratives posed to their society, to continuing peace, justice and stability in
a city in the sun, they were aware of the hidden hands creating imposed realities
in their kin that threatened a city in the sun, and all there was in it, aware they were, of the
realities manifest in those folks, the splitters, the entities that had subdued them, and the
forces that controlled them, they were not under any illusion nor were they deluded about
some digital versus biological self, they knew they were immaterial amalgams
with bits that fought for material expression in consciousnesses as a city in the sun.

There was no doubt in their minds about the chicaneries of the splitters and misinformation
they peddled aimed at socially engineering folks, paying them off entertaining them with

'exciting' news and games hammering into their heads propaganda such as the cellphone and the
peoples being one, a singularity, that the peoples were cyborgs, yet these splitters were ranting
about the 'socialism' they surreptitiously practiced, just to create a panic having
split political discourses, like everything else, into socialism, which they demonized,
and capitalism, which they hailed, but the peoples were no longer fooled by any doctrinal
ideological grand narrative, they all simply wanted to be free to chart the path to
a more perfect union and not to chicane to Eden's gate, if at all, the splitters any
notion had of even doing so, or if at all they could, treading an opposite route to Sheol.

The peoples had cleared their eyes of motes, they had seen the light illuminated in the sun, they were
no longer intimidated by grand narratives, they were no longer afraid of being fired from
their jobs if they criticized the boss, nor were they even afraid they might be incinerated
in the desert for not keeping quiet and simply obeying the orders given them by some
mules of some hidden hands, no, they were surer-footed in the world prepared to face their foes to keep
their reality clean, and free of miasmic contaminating realities, obnoxious
consciousnesses marauding spacetime pinching energy from unsuspecting 'folks,' or in quantum
mechanics parlance, wave fields of alliances of energy forms overwhelming other such
entities, stealing energy from them and, in doing so, becoming yea the predominant
consciousnesses manifest in the overall realities of the components of the mix.

Book 3

Yes, the peoples knew about the mix, about the amalgams, and about the consciousnesses of whose predominant components manifest in the reality they shared: and they did not want to lose their statuses as the predominant consciousnesses that indeed manifest the realities they shared, they were determined to see their world remain a city in the sun, they were set to do whatever it took to follow the path of goodness that led them to where they were, from where they intended to seek ascension yea to higher realms, ready they were to seek to be more perfect and to make their world more perfect for the good of all, why they were ever prepared to very closely examine every grand narrative some peoples were spreading in various ways such as on social media, in the news and on television, to be certain they were not undermining the hard-won safety, peace, joy, and justice evident in the city of the sun.

They didn't forget the roles grand narratives that played in blinding them to what was really going on in their precious world, the mind control their so-called leaders perpetrated to ensure they all remained in limbo, flustered by the mysteries all around them wary not of the processes yea that determined their realities and what to do about their limboed dissociated minds, they knew nothing about the nature and workings of angst that kept them inure to the so-called 'human condition' that they all went through no matter knight or knave; they remembered their struggles to figure what existence was about, and why they had to pay such a high premium for it in their world, suffering worrying to death anxious about whether or not they, in fact, existed and if so why they did, and whence they headed after they died: those were very difficult days for the folks, indeed, days they wished never came back to the city of the sun, days they knew might return.

Somewhere in their minds, the peoples realized they were exposed to the trickery of those among them that wanted to keep them as slaves for ever O yea, the peoples were aware of the so-called externalizations of the hierarchies of immaterial entities among them, what the peoples referred to as the heretofore predominant consciousnesses that manifest their realities, they knew that these folks were in league on a different agenda if even they professed to be on the same agenda as the rest of the peoples, but they were claiming to be experts at a game whose secrets the peoples had unveiled, if these splitters really believed they were fooling everyone else, playing their silly games, as the peoples saw them albeit always on their guards, to be certain the splitters never caught them off-guard with whatever novel tricks they were into, so, they were able to keep their city the way it was despite the ever-looming threats.

Doubtless, the peoples of a city in the sun were constantly under threat both from within and from outside their world, but they were all bent on maintaining their independence and warding off their erstwhile overlords, who appeared equally bent on returning the peoples into their spheres of influence, their hegemonic folds, the situation, perennially tense, one waxing and waning over time, the splitters gaining leverage at times, the lumpers, as the splitters liked to call the peoples, warding them off at other times, through all of which a city in the sun remained intact, the pearl of the realms as the peoples saw their city despite all the spleen vented on it, the envy of the voids wherein it stood higher than all the rest, the place where everyone wanted to be, a city where inequality did not exist a place where its institution had been torn down, where everyone played their part in forging an even better more perfect city, yea.

The tensions never ceased, as some of the peoples preferred the old distinctions between black and white
folks, the rich and the poor, women and men, straight and gay, and all manner of splitting society,
which the peoples had seen as a ploy to create animosity between the peoples and to
cause chaos and instability in society, scenarios they had all rejected
but which the splitters seemed they had to continue to use to achieve their goal of subjugating
the peoples once again, so, they kept drumming disparities into the heads of the peoples via
all sorts of media avenue, they infiltrated the schools and school system and created
divisions between teachers, between parents, between schools, even between students on whether to
teach creationism or evolution as being the origin of humankind for instance,
they infiltrated every aspect of society including its politics; everything.

No issue was off the table for the splitters who even attempted to provoke a 'civil
war' between opposing racial groups,' surreptitiously resurrecting inequality in
some form or another in the areas where they had control, stepping up their activities
from time to time, incrementally but relentlessly eating O yes into the fabric of
stability in society as the peoples struggled to resist their incursions into
a city under the sun, struggles that went on over many years, struggles that led to each group
digging deep into their modus operandi to reformulate their strategies and tactics,
and to revisit the roots of their world views to ensure they are up to date and applicable
to their respective objectives: the tension was slowly escalating, alliances yea were
appearing that were hitherto considered implausible, between moderates in either group.

Some splitters and lumpers were starting to collaborate on issues of common interest for
example, regarding the economy, a major area of contention that all the
collaborators deemed necessary to discuss with a view to arriving at some point of
agreement, a consensus that would work for both groups: the collaborative efforts seemed to be
a good starting point for resolving ingrained differences O yes, between alliances of
consciousnesses that manifest reality in a city under the sun, something that both
splitters and lumpers must have realized was inevitable anyway considering the
nature of the operations of the wave fields involved in the negotiations of the deals
regarding energy exchanges that led to an alliance or the other yes gaining the
upper hand in manifesting the alliances constituting the consciousnesses revealed.

Each group soon began to pay increasing attention to the negotiated nature of the
consciousnesses manifest as reality yes even in a city under the sun, the
portal of transmission of sustenance from a primal source, as some traditions yea affirm, the
energies of the primal intellect to which elements of the alliances in both the
groups termed the splitters and lumpers subscribed, revealing the heterogeneity of hidden hands
and of the peoples in their world, a notion antithetical to that of inequality
in void, with alliances made and lost in transient motions that left no time for any of
the negotiators to claim superiority over another one, O yes, a so-called
superiority, even if claimed by entrenched alliances such as the splitters that held
sway in the city, might be lost, as it was to an alliance of the peoples, united yes.

Yes, the peoples united wrenched power from their erstwhile overlords, erasing any notion
of superiority, the basis and precursor of inequality, O yes, itself,

the atavistic epigenetic epiphenomena manifest in dualistic
frameworks, such as black versus white peoples, and women versus men, for establishing and yes for
perpetrating hegemonies in void, one that brought the nature of reality to the fore,
one that spoke to the findings in their study that amalgams they all were and not some mixture of
dichotomous digital and biological entities, some technological array
a singularity wherein these two entities merged into some mattered entity called
cyborgs: this realization reinforced the varied nature of the components yes of the
amalgams that made some of the players in both groups see the need to negotiate and unite.

The feasibility of the prospects of reconfiguring their alliances increasingly
became clear to an increasingly tense world, hardliners on both sides stubbornly sticking to their
guns but many, in between, working together seeking a common ground, more pliable to the
idea of forgetting about whatever each meant by superiority and as one,
redefining the basis of interactive processes the consciousnesses of the product
of their alliances manifested as reality, as a city in the sun, so, things
started to change bit by bit in a city in the sun, under the aegis yea of the primal
energetic elements that sourced the sun, as some traditions believed, the peoples drifted in
the directions they felt most served their desire towards achieving their aim of being more perfect in
a negotiated state for peace to reign, or as things were, prepared yes to keep resisting change.

Book 4

A city in the sun soon began to show cleavages that portended a future that might not
be the same as again, one that was going to be much different from the one its peoples yanked
from their erstwhile overlords, and everyone knew it, even their foes, some of whom were already
working with like-minded folks across the isle to tread a common path, for the common good, having
erased the contentious notion of superiority as being mythical given yea the
propensities of energetic wave fields for fleeting unstable alliances no matter
yes how entrenched, an idea that the peoples earlier used to negotiate and remove
stifling grand narratives from the consciousnesses of their folks, which led to their unity, and their
ability to wrench power off the so-called hidden hands, an idea some constituents
of this hitherto 'monolithic' alliance of splitters also soon embraced; a new path, drawn.

The consciousnesses at the extreme ends in both groups continued to do business as before,
along the path of ascension and of destruction, but there were moderate consciousnesses that
realized they could achieve their respective goals that coincided in some way, the peoples in
this group realized they could achieve their goal of seeking ascension for themselves and for their world
without needing to be confrontational toward consciousnesses that was not in any way
confrontational towards them, consciousnesses that did not consider them inferior and
that did not see them as flotsams and jetsams to be treated unequally as slaves, as wretched
earthlings consciousnesses that, therefore, had no need to ram any grand narrative yes down their throats,
consciousnesses that wanted to live in peace and harmony with every other consciousness and
they were set to engage in energy exchanges in a fair and civil manner in their world.

The moderates in the group that some referred to as lumpers were, therefore, comfortable reaching
a consensus with some of their erstwhile foes, the realities that ensued pretty much like their
penultimate reality, albeit with the actions of the consciousnesses yes at both
extremes still uncompromising those erstwhile overlords still determined to regain full control
over the peoples, a situation that those at the extremes of the so-called lumpers doubtless
absolutely rejected, and that did not mean that any of the peoples wanted to ever
be slaves, some of them, however, did not think the door must be closed to anyone seeking peace, and
who did not want to control them: so did a city in the sun operated in a very
delicate balance for some years, meanwhile, still under major threats from within and without its shared
realities, uncertain everyone was how long it would take for the balance to tip over.

This was an important consideration for all parties, moderate or extreme, they all indeed
realized that their transactional games were pivoted on the success of their alliances,
in other words, that they were predicated on alliances to begin with, at a certain
level, alliances of configurations and reconfigurations of wave fields yes, with
capacities, in some cases, to materialize from resultant consciousnesses that were
viable in a voided spacetime as the city in a sun they knew, alliances that were
inherently unstable and were prone to disintegrating, in some cases, no sooner than
they were formed and, in any case, that did not produce immortal mattered forms, such as the human
forms, wherein the amalgams of alliances referred to as humans operated in the
multilevel shared realities they struggled to control, in bids rooted in their backroom deals.

Yes, they knew their struggle to control their shared realities were rooted in the behind-the-scenes immateriality, as the hidden hands, in which the transactions occurred: they all knew these things and worried to death as to what it meant for their very existence, for the notion of the 'immortality of the soul' they sought in their varied ways, a state which, for some meant ascension to yoke with ane and, for others, to sustain an ouroboros wolfing peoples, yea, so, they were yes all concerned about survival albeit for reasons as varied as their shapes and their forms, their potentially mattered forms that ranged from anything to anything, you know, from popping pumpkins to sticks, you know, vectors, to ants, snakes, little green peoples, shimmering very amorphous entities, and humanoid beings, so they worried, they worried about surviving, if even at one another's expense, which meant they had to form alliances, shifting alliances, yes.

They knew they had to form alliances, reach some sort of consensus, all the time, why the peoples in the city in a sun knew they were constantly under threat, as indeed, their erstwhile bosses, former overlords intent on being overlords again, also knew they were constantly under threat, from alliances in the realms, all over the realms, considerations that played major roles in the configurations and reconfigurations that shaped reshaped a city in the sun, determined what later happened to the consciousnesses that made up the peoples and those that made up their erstwhile bosses yea, as shifting alliances led to the balance of forces tipping so wildly, enough at last to result in a seismic shift in how transactions occurred behind the scenes in a city in the sun, it was a huge paradigmatic shift that everyone, in all probability, saw coming, given the increasing recognition of the values lost.

Yes, the values of alliances, even of foes, they lost due to developments in the realms, what appeared to be some atavistic tendencies for consciousness to yes, incrementally debase, the farther from the base, from the primal portal manifest in the sun which indeed, might explain the formation of alliances that betrayed the plan, intention of the peoples to embrace the light, illuminated, to pursue the path of righteousness to have a chance yes to enter Eden's gate, that metaphoric grove that signaled ascension yea, revealed cryptic codes, some sacred glyphs and sundry formalized axioms that secreted mysteries of life in a void, a voided spacetime a grove that led them to being more perfect, and being able to more perfect make their consciousnesses manifest in realities they shared: they might well be, you know, some hex, not hex, okay, but some interactive manner that increasingly contaminated the 'goodness.'

The goodness of the primal source, that is, inherent tendencies towards the blind pursuit yes of survival, or even immortality for its own sake, rather than a concerted effort yea to attain salvation in the background of cut-throat energy-exchange transactions that some anaconda hosted in a voided spacetime; and, indeed, these tendencies might be other things 'external' to the alliances but inherent O yes in the participants in all the alliances, namely, an unstoppable entropy that led to increasing disorder that rendered the consciousnesses and their begotten realities ever more flawed, yet which, that this city in the sun became a paradise, like a phoenix, triumphantly rose from the ashes of atavistic immolation, might contend, debunked or, maybe be better still, rendered as not being inevitable a path the accretion of their realities must tread, yea affirmed.

In other words, that there was always a path to salvation opened to any consciousness that with, whatever little agency it had, chose the path of goodness, worked hard to ascension yea

attain, many in a city in the sun realized, which might explain the willingness of some
of them to work with folks across the isle, if even former foes, something that might have reduced the
overall impact of the negativity that typified the alliances prevalent
in the void, from which the peoples freed themselves took control of their lives, created a city in
the sun, a healthy and prosperous alliance of consciousnesses where peace, joy, and justice reigned,
prevailed over negativities that other consciousnesses purveyed: the willingness to form
alliances regardless of the doctrinal or ideological leanings of players
in the alliances formed the spine of values that served the city well, created avenues.

It created avenues for mutually beneficial commerce with sundry players in
the realms, with entities from near and far with goodwill in their hearts, yet this situation was not
to last forever as, this time, the peoples slipped, and the forces that had relentlessly threatened
them, and their alliance partners, again, gained the upper hand, in a dramatic turn of events
with insidious roots yea in targeted misinformation, information asymmetry,
propaganda and indeed, in the resurgence of grand narratives among peoples that perhaps
PP1, protein phosphatase one seemed to be doing a number on their memories, or that
perhaps had too much of the Lethe to drink: the loss of virtuousness a very traumatic turn
of events verily created for the peoples and their alliances, evident in the
events in the city yea, after the power shift that brought negativity out of the crypts.

Book 5

T hings changed very quickly in the city as, apparently, carefully planned and executed
assaults on the peoples' emotions and intellect, began to take their toll on the populace,
with indoctrination programs reinvigorating latent grand narratives, and conspiracy
theories grew exponentially fueling fear, creating divisions among the folks,
with the peoples diving for cover in their prior comfort zones, among their former 'group think' friends,
succor-seeking they became headed for their previous schemas, the grand narratives they embraced
before they won the war against their former lords in void: many of the peoples gradually
lost faith in the ability of their leaders to see them through the difficulties they were all
experiencing as their returning overlords re-instituted the tools they used in the
past to oppress the peoples and advantage one group over another stoking divisions yea.

There were also sorts of wars, drug wars, proxy wars, and nameless wars, there was chaos everywhere in
a city in the sun turned into a city in the dark as gloom descended on the city
and as ravens roamed the streets the 'broomed ones' regularly met at midnight at the crossroads yea,
life became a chore economic downturns recessions brought, extreme poverty took centre stage
as people lost their jobs, protests and riots led to wanton property damage, outbreaks of viral
infections led to serious illnesses that overwhelmed the health systems, nothing just seemed to
be working right, meanwhile, inequality and its manifestations such as income gap, and
gender disparity, and racial divisions, and bigotry in every sense including yes,
religious fascism, was rife, and worsening, a lot of things that was supposed to be extinct,
things the younger generations never even knew existed suddenly began to crop up.

This hitherto sunny city was no longer sunny: it was filled with agony, tears and woes,
many, seeking to know why and how things turned so ugly, so fast, the answers they proffered, legion,
as many and diverse as the questions asked and, given the state of knowledge in society,
with the peoples being highly educated and conversant with the mechanics of the goings
on in their world, among the reasons they were all flabbergasted to be, as it seemed, caught off guard
by their foes, some of whom, in fact, had been collaborating with the peoples for many years, to
find mutually acceptable solutions to the problems they all faced, primarily, the
issue of inequality that they agreed was the root cause of the major contentions and
of chaos in society, collaborations that appeared to have gone well, but which some of the peoples were
saying were espionage operations by their foes, disguised as collaborations, of friends.

Matters got to the point where everyone started to suspect everyone else as being spies, as being
saboteurs, and traitors, a city in the sun was slowly turning into a theatre of very
paranoid consciousnesses pretending to be one united entity, whereas they were all
forming little cliques and alliances to destroy one another even family brewing
trouble within the family and with 'outsiders' drumming the beats of war, the idea being that
it was difficult to know who was in alliance with their foes, in effect, hard to tell who was
a friend and who was a foe; and matters only got worse with time, more so as the predominant
alliance of consciousnesses that controlled the manifest reality only more potent
became, its success in dividing and ruling the peoples, unprecedented and, perhaps might
have astounded them, even them, the experts at forging deals, cut-throat deals to ensure they survived.

Indeed, these self-proclaimed experts of deals, of brutal energy-exchanges at all costs, to be sure that they kept the snake alive in a voided space, might have been surprised that they so totally routed the peoples who seemed to be in disarray, and if even they were not surprised, that they achieved their goal of regaining control over peoples they regarded as their slaves must have pleased them a lot, and revamped their malevolence towards their former slaves, a very sad turn yea of events for peoples that had tasted freedom from serfdom, seen peace and prosperity, peoples that had vowed never to find themselves in a slavery situation ever again, it was quite disappointing and sad that they let the balance of alliances between positivity and negativity tip against them, as a result of which they landed back in slavery days, something some of them continued to ascribe to an atavistic hex, others to the void.

Yes, the void as the reality of the manifest consciousnesses we share, which is subject to the inevitable progression of entropy, that indeed, any consciousness yea or alliances of consciousnesses mattered in void must expect, yet, many more remained very skeptical about the notion of allowing splitters in their midst, many were still wary of collaborating with wave fields with diametrically opposite agendas, in the main, regardless they were able to find common grounds regarding issues of interest to both the lumpers and the splitters, the collaborations among the so-called moderates on both sides in progress, albeit, significantly scaled down, so, views were diverse and often conflictual among the peoples, fueled, at least in part, by the infusion of disruptive energies as data and information that created cognitive dissonance among the peoples, O yes.

Questions arose among the peoples regarding what they needed to do going forward, how they could regain the power they lost, and be free to make choices unfettered once again, more so as they knew what damage somehow, the barrages of fake, withheld and misrepresented data and information constantly replicated in their world caused in the consciousnesses of the peoples, one of the first issues they agreed they must address to even start to consider yes, any other steps that they needed to take to reacquire the values they lost, which regained, they deemed would redirect them to the path of ascension they previously treaded, something that would make it harder for them to buy the chicanery of expert tricksters that might be posing as friends and collaborators, and easier to coalesce opinions among the many factions into which they, the so-called lumpers had split, so, they were regrouping to act, once again.

Meanwhile, the city's wounds festered, corruption raged, autocracy prevailed, sit-tight leaders reigned like monarchs nothing was the same, the power-that-was turned the peoples on one another demonized immigrants the weak and the poor, and the disadvantaged peoples that mostly constituted the weak and the poor, the institutions and policies that perpetrated inequality waxed stronger and seemed unstoppable, even as many in the advantaged groups had yea seen through the facade of inequality, even as it was supposed to be harder for the overlords to sell their thesis-antithesis-synthesis dialectic to divide and conquer yea the peoples, even with all these issues to contend with, the overlords could care less about their deeds, about creating more vicious oppressive instruments to keep the peoples in line as their slaves for aye, after all, they had cremated care, they had no morals, no ethics, no empathy; sad.

Matters went from bad to worse, the peoples struggled to persuade their members to see the 'bosses' as invaders of their consciousnesses for what they were, parasites controlling their cognitive

faculties, yes a way to express the manifestations of consciousness in the language of
a mattered state, for the biological forms in which they manifested in the world they knew
was simply that, mattered accretions of atavistic epigenetic epiphenomena,
so, they spoke the 'shared language' of a shared reality, an invasion of their minds, O yes,
the shenanigans of their overlords, whoever or whatever they were which, by the way they
had also made up their minds about, they knew were wave fields like themselves that however appeared to
prefer being in cognito, which itself suggested they had things to hide, which required that they did
not openly matter their consciousnesses, but operate them yea in those of their mattered hosts.

The peoples were slow to respond to this plea to review their 'cherished' beliefs, the constricting grand
narratives that historically held them down was at it again, and this time, with a venom,
perhaps to make the peoples pay for escaping the slave yards, breaking free of the iron grips in
a snaky void, perhaps for other reasons best known to the bosses, to the parasites, so, the
peoples were slow to embrace notions of tossing the grand narratives, even knowing they were made
to control their minds, they were reluctant to use the little agency they had to break free like
they did in the past, or they might have been unable so to do held down much tighter yea, but they
seemed to be buying in into the notion little by little over time, perhaps they had all,
united, started to forge ever stronger alliances, perhaps the alliances they were
forging made the difference, and they might be on track to turn the tide against their bosses, again.

Book 6

It was beginning to look like the peoples might be making progress in their bid to be free again, the need for them to embrace eclectic perspectives on goings on the city, crystal clear to them, a situation they relished as they pondered what mathematical Adinkras woven
into their reality meant for their ideas of hidden hands operational as
computer simulations in the consciousness crypts, or put differently, in alliances
of ghosts! Yes, the elusiveness of consciousness, 'situated,' wherever, spoke to the prospects
of knowledge of the mysteries of the world no longer exclusively in the hands of the so-
called keepers of the secrets of the gods, and to the nature of consciousness being overarching,
within which resided computer codes woven into the fabric of reality, yea in
a voided spacetime shared in the city as was the case wherever else in void, in life revealed.

Yet, the peoples knew they were struggling, the peoples knew they had a formidable foe, or indeed
foes, they knew they faced accretions of atavistic alliances that kept growing bigger right
afore their very eyes, consciousnesses miasmic operating in the city's nooks and in
all its crannies in the name yes of a supreme being of grand narratives unimodal spread in
sundry hues, they continued to seek knowledge from eclectic sources to better figure out the
operations of this mammoth alliance of alliances that bestrode their world, whose sole and
ultimate goal appeared to be to exert control over every consciousness in the realm, the
peoples concluded as they did in the past, a goal they resisted, succeeded in trashing, then
lost, for reasons they felt created an urgent need for exploring what they needed to do be
free again, to be able to pursue their goal of making their consciousness more perfect, O yes.

They searched everywhere wondering what was really going on, trying their darnedest to comprehend
the real motives of their foes, the giants that trampled upon them in all sorts of ways, they wondered
what transformations their nemesis had undergone atavistically since they all last freed
themselves from a serfdom that appeared increasingly harder to escape than it was, to escape,
a task that must be done, they wondered how this consciousness was able to garner the combined strength
of elements of its hierarchies, more so, its leaders, and its populist majority yes,
despite their objectives not being exactly coalesced, the higher echelons keener on politico-economic gains
whereas the populist majority were keener on demonstrated sinew, strength, power yea
over others, if even tyrannical, murderous, unconscionable, just power, yes raw
power, which they claimed was consistent with their doctrine, ideology or theology, yoo.

So, the peoples reckoned that perhaps these ostensibly doctrinal cum economic gap yes
between the leaders and the masses in the alliances of consciousnesses they all had to
reckon with was no gap after all, at least, assuming that the leaders wanted economic
power to have political clout, yes, strength, power, the same strength the populist elements in
the alliances craved, and wanted spread at home, and as domestic policy couched as foreign
policy abroad: both groups wanted strength, power wielded on their behalf over others yea in
a voided spacetime in a city in the sun: this seemed to the peoples to be the crux of the
matter, the answer perhaps to the question of what their overlords really wanted, power, but
to what end? They asked! Survival? But for what reason, more so, as they were using their power for
all sorts of 'unholy' reasons, firing people that dared challenge them from their jobs, behaving crazed.

Yes, why were the oppressors keen to have so much strength, why did they prefer to tryst with tyrants and dictators why did they form alliances with fascists why did they support patently evil deeds, did they do these things just because they demonstrated that these evil entities and their deeds had shown strength by craving and deploying 'strength,' consistent with their ideology? Was that why they would obey any command by anything that ordered them to refuse to wear face masks in a pandemic, a view that suggested they would rather have everyone dead! Lord have mercy, yes, many of the peoples must have said, alarmed, whenever such thoughts crossed their minds, an alarm any of them must have considered a trigger to act on, one that must have very likely stirred them to action to do whatever they could to achieve their goal, one likely to have emboldened them to take back power from their wicked bosses free themselves of pain, of mental torture, as slaves, in void.

So, the peoples started to see why their so-called overlords were empowered to say and do all sorts of things to undermine others and society, with ignominy, why they were turning people into mules, and depriving them of their lives and livelihoods at will, and as the peoples dug deeper, they realized how their overlords seemingly effortlessly controlled the other consciousnesses whether or not they were constituents of alliances of splitters or of lumpers in their world. and determined what they manifested and what they did not: they discovered that the reign of terror of their bosses had gotten even worse as also had the means by which they conducted their autocratic agendas, they found out how much easier it had been for these things to demand and obtain total surrender from everyone else they considered yes, too disgusting even to touch, including members of their so-called alliances, which was instructive.

It was indeed, instructive, it further opened the eyes of the peoples to how they could hope to achieve their aim, namely, by digging much deeper into the drivers of the activities of these entities that even split their so-called alliance members to force them to remember the point of consensus, namely, strength, the acquisition and maintenance of power over all else, and verily, the demand for total surrender from everyone else, the establishment of an autocratic hegemony over the entire world in alliance with others in the league strategically placed in different corners of the void, to have the entire void yes, permanently in their grips, yet the question remains: to what end? Why would these entities want to have the entire void under their control? Could it be to finally and totally erase all traces of secularism? But why? Could it be to ensure some deep secrets remained so?

The peoples were struggling to get to the bottom of the mysteries of humanity which, they increasingly felt was being protected by a cabal of autocratic entities that wanted to have exclusive access to these secrets with which they bamboozled everyone, and planned to continue to use to befuddle everyone else, pretty much like the Copernican days of yore when the earth was the centre of the universe and any dissenter risked being burnt at the stake, a line of thought even the toughest among the peoples cringed from, perhaps not because they were at all afraid to burn in hell, but because they were struck by the increasing tendency of the progression of happenings in their world towards those dark ages in the history yea of humanity, a throwback hundreds of years into gloom, presided over by some nasty bugs.

The deeper they dug the more questions arose, including what secrets they kept and why they did not want others to know what they were, apparently, not even the mathematicians in the realms were exempt: so why? Was there something going on outside the energy-exchanges of wave fields that, indeed, explained the voracious appetites of these entities for, at it surely appears, assorted energy types, with preferences for certain types of consciousnesses mattered in the void, as this or that form of humans, perhaps across the life cycle, perhaps related to gender or to colour or the so-called races of peoples? Could this be why they had the wicked hierarchical structures that meant they could consider those in the lower rungs of the ladder, disgusting even to touch, and why they had such rigid control over them that they could not dare to think on their own, and if they did, faced the wrath of the Leviathan yea?

Questions such as these helped the peoples of a city in the sun to better figure the reasons the behemoth that controlled them was able to snatch back control from them and to plunge them into their miserable descent from grace to grass and, even more importantly as they claimed, to see clearly and understand the seriousness of the hold that their controllers had over the minds of their folks who appeared fanatical about the grand narratives peddled by overlords to hold them down, locked in for aye in Platonic caves, figure what to do to regain control over the lives as individuals and, collectively, their city, that they would be able yea to redirect themselves along the path of virtue, goodness and perfection seek ascension yea to Eden free to take decisions on their own, able to chart their chosen paths to achieve their aim, afraid not to seek to escape from the belly of a snake, from fangs of an ouroboros, yea.

Book 7

They were no longer in the dark as much as before, they made it a priority thenceforth to persuade their members to see the damage to their minds the entities that controlled the void yes behind the scenes were inflicting not only to keep them enslaved but also to prevent them from participating in the efforts to united be to rid their world of bugs, from demonic intelligences holding everyone to ransom for a bowl of rice, dumbing everyone down entertaining them to distract them from thinking about what was really going on yea in their precious world, pretty much like in the days of the gladiators Roman elites used to keep the ruled from rising up against their rulers, talk about socialism! So, the peoples embarked on forming their own little cliques, their own little alliances using the little agencies they had to help their folks check how things were and to see through the 'facts' that were actually fiction, O yes.

With time, things began to slowly change, and the grand narratives came under the peoples' kliegs again, people were openly asking questions about who or what the controllers of the void were and what they were into and wanted, the younger ones were becoming increasingly agitated over what they saw as the mortgaging of their lives by their so-called leaders and demanding change, they demanded changes to the establishments not only in the city in the sun yes but also in other parts of the void: there were protests everywhere, protestors demanded justice and equality everywhere in void, things were slowly but surely falling apart everywhere the externalized hierarchies clearly in disarray, and it appeared the worst nightmares of the bosses were unfolding before their very eyes, that their hegemony was in shambles yes as factions began to emerge in their ranks, engaged in doctrinal and sundry feuds, their world, ablaze.

The world of the splitters unraveled quickly as the infighting blew open and it became clear that their purported commitment to 'strength' they avowed their credos promoted was being played out in the open among themselves, cracks in their alliances gaping wider over time, everyone not unwary of the increasing vulnerability of the overlords that held sway in their void, controlled their thoughts, their actions and indeed, their lives, entities yes that empowered and indeed strengthened institutional structures of oppression that split their world in bits, stoked internecine conflicts all over the void, forces and processes as historicism described them that yes determined and influenced the void and were beyond the control of the peoples therein in the world, all falling apart: the peoples watched these developments with keen interest and became ever more vigilant to be sure they did not miss any chance to regain control of their void, O yes.

The peoples continued to work hard to take back their lives from consciousnesses that were hellbent of keeping them as slaves and nothing else, using them as energy sources forever in a void, yes in spacetime forming alliances configuring reconfiguring realities, of individuals as individuals and in association with others in the void, collectively, making sure everything and everyone danced to their tunes, ensuring their cryptic agendas were met was clearly the most important thing they cared about, no matter the cost to whoever they needed to meet these agendas yea, regardless millions lost their lives yes in the process, obeying for instance the orders of some so-called leader of the 'group think' entities they engineered in grand narratives they intended to ram down everybody's throat, of course with the active execution of their plan by the 'dress-up' fellows, consciousnesses robed, O yes.

Yes, dressed up in funny togas to create an aura of whatever, knowing not naked they
were in the eyes of the peoples who had seen through their skins, folks who had known how they operated
how, operationally, consciousnesses were not as complicated as they seemed, as they made
themselves out to be to perpetuate the fear they had instilled in the peoples since the days of
yore since time immemorial O yea, a devilish act that they continued to try to keep
instilling in all the peoples but were clearly hitting a very solid rock indeed in the
determination of the peoples to never be slaves again, peoples who had gleaned the secrets
these mules secreted under their mass-produced dross that were their ilks in their consciousness assembly
lines: yes, the peoples were waking up from their slumber deep and seeing the light, becoming
illuminated once again, they were seeing through the facade of the 'dress-up' guys, at last.

They were seeing the fish, they were seeing the snakes they were seeing the secrets hidden in their void,
in plain sight, and asking questions yea, a whole set of questions answers to which they found albeit
in bits and pieces yea, from sources eclectic useful nuggets of data gems they were able
to put together into actionable information to advance their cause, they were seeing
a lot of things and were one another see these things, they were increasingly convinced they would
triumph, once again, in their struggles against the forces of darkness that wanted to enslave them
all forevermore in void in the belly of a snake, they were able to persuade their kin
to clear their eyes of motes that had re-occupied their eyes blinding them to the nature of their world they
had found when they broke free of bugs, denounced alliances they had hobnobbing with the scaly ones
and chose to take decisions on their own, when they chose the path of righteousness evil decried.

It took a long time for them to break free of slavery yea: they never forgot that, which had them
asking questions regarding why they slipped back into their evil ways, why they gave up their city
in the sun for one in utter darkness, and they realized how pernicious signing up with the
devil could be, how these aberrant trickster consciousnesses were on a mission to harvest yes,
unsuspecting souls, and nothing more, they did again on closer scrutiny of the steadily
incremental findings of their study, their unrelenting efforts to figure out their lives in
a city in the sun, and more questions kept coming, and they embraced them, sought to answer them the
best they could, using the answers they found to help one another break free of the shackles of the
information cage wherein, like some lost birds, they were kept, incarcerated like criminals on
death row awaiting their turn to be wolfed, criminals accused, judged, and sentenced to death by the boss.

Yes, whoever or whatever this so-called boss was: the peoples were able to help one another
to toss the dross: there was no gem there, only rut, and that was increasingly clear to them, they
realized their options were to free themselves of slavery or live and die as slaves for ever
in an ouroboros for eternity, the latter option, more and more of them did not at
all even consider, they did not even consider kowtowing to very malevolent
alliances lording it over them and they did not consider not doing something to change
their ugly mental state, but they knew they had to be nimble and be cryptic about their plan to
take back their lives from some crazy bug, so, they kept persuading their folks to get out of their deals
with demonic entities operating in their world feeding them daily with skewed data and
information with fake news doctored news whatever news that fed their crazy minds to kill the folks O yes.

So, the peoples were determined not to be slaughtered, like rats, they were prepared to follow the pied
piper out of town, metaphorically, they were sure they would die of hunger otherwise in

a city in the dark, that had only more than enough food for some people to eat and none for
everyone else, absolutely none, after all, they, the famished, were the food, the sources yea of
energy that kept the snake alive, why they could die in numbers killed by some bug or virus or
whatever to be born again, why the secularist could go to hell, and if they chose yea to
agitate about some abortion thing, risked being put in the hottest part of hell, where those guilty
of sedition went, so, the peoples were set to leave spiritually bankrupt realities,
for good, and were set to employ their consciousnesses to forge the reality of a city
in the sun, they were set to redirect themselves and tread the path of goodness, to a higher ground.

Meanwhile, the alliances of the forces of darkness were crumbling faster than before, and it
seemed some members of these alliances were also realizing how 'disgusting' in the eyes
of their transactionally-minded leaders they were, they were also starting yes, to see through the
veneer of 'holiness' presented to them, they had begun to see that the 'noumena' of the
phenomena they embraced, or better put, that they were coerced to embrace with promises of
'immortality' or whatever was the exact opposite, of the phenomena that they
embraced, in the main, if even flawed, in other words, these folks actually embraced the notion
that they were, like everyone else, inherently flawed, and sought salvation in their trusted credos,
not realizing that the purveyors of the credos reflections of the evil 'noumena'
were, something that was increasingly obvious to some of them to such an extent that they ran.

Book 8

Yes, these 'disgruntled' members, as their erstwhile alliances tagged them, literally ran away from the alliances they considered inconsistent with their faith, and yes, they all openly rebelled against their alliances and joined the alliances of the peoples trying to free themselves of the chicanery of the demonic cohorts lording it over everyone in void, carrying on as if they were invincible, and as if they were above the law and could do whatever they liked, which had many in the void, including former members of their almost defunct alliances, hitherto regarded as moderate splitters, and who had worked with the moderate lumpers in the past, asking what made them so confident that they trampled on people, everyone and everything with impunity and, apparently, got away with it, questions that the peoples felt needed answering as part of the information they needed for their plans.

The peoples deemed answers to the question regarding possible hidden entities backing their hidden overlords, important for their strategies of regaining freedom from their so-called lords, to work so, they worked hard at finding the answers and searched everywhere for clues and they dug ever deeper into their sources to be certain they left no stone unturned, as the sages used to say, they established cross-alliances as they restarted collaborating with all the rebels, erstwhile alliances across the isle, the moderate splitters, they sought information yea from wherever they could, and they got information, data and information, some of which added to what their study already said, others brand new, they found out about the multiplicity of voids that the constituents of their amalgams might have come from, some of them near and others very far away, these sundry locations not all the same regarding their characteristics.

They were also different regarding their missions, with some manifested as mattered states while others, immaterial remained yet able to influence goings on in void, the ones by consensus they referred to as inter dimensional entities that, as opposed yea to the inter galactics, did not need to engage in energy-exchanges and did not at all trade in any forms of energy in other words, were self-sufficient super intelligent beings, entities that sought peace for all in paradise, showed everyone that it was possible yes to attain perfection enter Eden's gate; and their negatively-oriented counterparts, yea. The peoples and their collaborators were soon to find out the important roles that these deeper entities played in their affairs, entities, or as they concluded, super-consciousnesses in other hierarchical structures, this time, internalized, that indeed controlled externalized beings.

As such, they found out that their so-called bosses had bosses over which they had no control, because the super-intelligent internalized hierarchies had no need for the energies that the intergalactic entities exchanged to stay alive, so, it seemed the entities that exchanged energy to stay alive could undergo metamorphosis in either of the directions of the inter dimensional entities to become inter dimensional too, either yes along the path of ascension engaged in goodness and a quest for more perfection, or in yes badness and a quest for more imperfection, helped along which path, yea the inter dimensional internalized entities operating in the void, the peoples and their collaborators noted, agreeing that the answer they sought regarding the hidden forces behind the actions of their hidden bosses were inter dimensional beings in internalized hierarchical 'forms.'

So, these internalized, simply meaning they were hidden from the externalized, hierarchies, had
the ability to help the externalized hierarchies achieve O yes their goals of either
apotheosizing or demonizing their consciousnesses mattered in void, which could explain
the obscene wickedness evident in void, the perpetrators of which were goaded on yes by
inter dimensional entities that resided in the darkest depths of the abyss, reckoned
the peoples and their friends, why these perpetrators appeared not to care about whose ox was gored by
their shenanigans and evil machinations in a void, why they even seemed emboldened to
escalate their evilness as they got away with prior evil deeds, the peoples and their friends
happy they were getting closer and closer to the truth of what was happening to them and to
their precious city in the sun, so, they continued to work on knowing even more, on their lords.

They wanted to know more about their overlords and about their interactions with the inter
dimensional beings, they wanted to know whether these 'untouchable' inter dimensional being
or entities actively or only passively played any role in their predicament, if
they only guided consciousnesses that had shown an interest in travelling yes in their own
direction or offered unsolicited assistance to veer consciousnesses in their preferred
direction, the latter which they already knew the externalized hierarchies did that wanted
to travel in either direction, pretty much as they were doing persuading their folks to
jettison grand narratives that held them down and turn away from evilness to live a very
virtuous life, they were keen to know if these inter dimensional entities would try to stop
consciousnesses choosing which path they wanted to tread and redirect them towards 'heaven' or 'hell.'

They wanted to know if the purveyors of Heaven and Hell engaged in solicitations, as
this yea would amount to, perhaps to fill up each of those abodes: they were keen to know a lot of
things, even rest assured they had once escaped the iron grips of their wicked overlords, broke free
of life in hell, so they kept digging, hoping to find answers to their queries as they did before,
and with a little help from their friends things started shaping up, and they started to put two and two
together and they were getting four, at least they knew they did not have Ganser syndrome, and were not
deluded about ferreting immaterial entities that they believed controlled their world,
they kept on digging, incrementally arriving at conclusions they never imagined could
be relevant to their quest, the expectations of the inter dimensional entities of
the choices consciousnesses made that could make them actively participate in worldly affairs.

Yes, the peoples and their friends concluded that the super-intelligences were indeed not at
all simply independent observers of what was going on in void, and that they intervened
at some level and at some point which, in effect, set up scenarios for what they all agreed
to call paradise wars, the paradise of goodness versus its enemies that dwelt in the deep
abyss of evilness, why there would be such wars though was a different matter that also called
for inquiries, the peoples and their friends figured the answers they got might make it easier for
their folks still entangled in grand narratives to free themselves of these grand narratives over them,
so, they kept digging to see if they would find any reason at all for super-intelligent
internalized hierarchical structures of inter dimensional entities to go to war with one another over
the choices less intelligent externalized hierarchical structures intergalactic, made.

They pondered this issue and hoped for an answer if even they were not sure yea they were indeed
asking the right question, given they were themselves engaged in a war of good versus evil in

their void trying to free themselves of the pervasive wickedness in void that robbed them of control
of their beloved city in the sun, control for which they were yet to reestablish and were
working hard so to do, and given that they believed apotropaic forces helped them to wrench
control from their overlords in the past and would help them do so again, in effect, tacitly
admitting to the fact that inter-dimensional entities interceded on their behalf
to win the war against the bugs, against 'spiritual wickedness in high places' as Paul said
in his epistle to the Ephesians, in effect, saying that these forces of goodness must have
fought against the forces of badness at the inter dimensional level, the high places yea.

The peoples and their friends concluded that the high places could not have been a lesser level than
the inter dimensional level and that, in any case, if even they were fighting with
intergalactic entities, not only, O yes, would the more potent inter dimensional
entities have easily defeated the intergalactic forces, but the latter would not
have been able to retake power from the inter dimensional forces, let alone, even
unfazed continue with their nasty habits of perpetrating wickedness in a voided space,
so the study continued, the matter of the active involvement of inter dimensional
entities in world affairs, settled, the next logical step in the view of the peoples and their
friends being to figure out what the aims of these inter dimensional entities were, why they would
actively intervene in the affairs of 'lesser beings,' an intriguing question they reckoned.

Book 9

It was not going to be easy to find the answer to the question regarding the reasons
that inter dimensional entities would actively and directly intervene in worldly
affairs, and it was not going to be just a matter of simply wanting to populate yea
heaven or hell, as if there was a party going on there: no it wasn't, they figured, but they
were all determined to probe the matter and to find the answers to the question, verily were
they yea attuned to possibilities that had emerged from their study but they talked about much
more than possibilities, they talked about the probabilities of the options they indeed,
considered actually occurring, for example, of the recognition by good inter
dimensional entities to identify who or what to fight for, an example being if
or not to fight for a 'virtuous' person that advised against wearing face masks in pandemics.

So, they did not expect good inter dimensional entities to support tricksters, charlatans,
or anyone not committed to treading the path of virtue and cared nothing about making
the void a better place for the good of all, they did not expect them to fight for purveyors of
grand narratives that did not practice what they professed, for whom precept trumped example, they did not
think that persons that coerced their followers they, nonetheless, referred to as disgusting to touch,
into taking decisions inimical to their health and wellbeing, and they did not think that the
inter dimensional entities would support persons that wilfully deprived others of their
means of livelihoods simply for having contrary views, the peoples and their friends could not even
imagine the inter dimensional entities waging a paradise war because of some
person that had no remorse over doing evil things and had no intention to mend their ways.

So, the folks had some notions regarding the circumstances inter dimensional entities
would likely wage a paradise war on someone's behalf, bad inter dimensional entities
for example livelier to support the opposite of the above scenarios, which they
realized brought them closer to answering the original question regarding what made their
overlords so confident about all the evil deeds they carried out, if there were in fact some
hidden entities backing them, giving them the audacity to do all those evil things, yes
even thinking they could gun someone down in broad daylight on a city street and nothing at all,
would happen to them, they would get away with it, so, the peoples and their friends felt some relief that
their overlords probably had the backing O yes of some demonic inter dimensional
entities to be able to act with such impunity and have everyone cowering, afraid.

It must be strange to even have to imagine people hiding in their closets when their so-called
leaders roared in rage, but the not only did, but also knew what precisely they were really up
against, 'spiritual wickedness in high places,' yet, they knew they were not alone, they knew the
good inter dimensional entities had their backs, they knew apotropaic forces moated
them, they knew aluta continua, and they were ready, along with their friends from across the
isle, so, they pressed on, continued to persuade their friends to open their minds to new vistas the
answers to their questions presented to them, their prospects of reaching Eden's gate, to enter where
they truly wanted to be, in Eden yea O yea, a metaphoric 'place' of excellence their
consciousnesses begot, where they were willing to mend their errant ways to be able yes to reach,
resolved to tread the path of virtue whence they headed yea, a more perfect union, sought, O yes.

With these in mind they continued with their efforts to free themselves of fangs of snakes, they were sure in
their minds they said that victory for them was not in doubt and all they needed to do was to be
patient and methodical in their ways, in particular to look back to see where and when they
lost their way in the city in the sun that that would not repeat the errors that they made: they all
realized they had no option, short of throwing their hands up in the air and resigning up with
the devil, than to tread the path of righteousness ascension to attain, headed they were at last
for Eden's gate aided by good inter dimensional entities yea along the way, they knew
their mistakes, that they got carried away by success after success in the city in the sun,
the envy of the rest of their world, a status they cherished and ballyhooed in realms, pride that in
part, eventually led to their downfall, a mistake they vowed to never ever make, again.

The situation with their bosses was deteriorating every day, confusion filled the
air their leadership in utter disarray, but despite and perhaps because of all these chaos,
negativity sure remained their game, more devilish were their ways, their focus yes on creating
disharmony than otherwise in void, and they seemed to be experts at doing so, perhaps not
caring about losing their control over everyone else, perhaps in the deluded belief
that nothing like that could ever happen to them again, believing that they had tightened all the
loopholes and were certain to have kept everyone in line, certain no alliances of foes, of
consciousnesses in void were strong enough to topple their hegemonies, and that in fact they had
overwhelming public opinion in their corner and were ever strong, forever would hold
sway in the void, so it was business as usual with the overlords, evermore depraved.

On the other hand the peoples were gaining ground as more and more of their folks were returning to
the fold, taking decisions on their own to lead a righteous life, rejecting errant ways, choosing
the path to excellence to be more perfect made their aims, more of them started to see the games their
bosses played, the chicanery of their so-called leaders leading them all astray, they began to
see the divide-and-rules tactics the bosses utilized that led them to affrays, when they all prayed
for peace, they saw the seeming 'changes' to societal structures that inequalities entrenched,
tho window dressings that they know could never change the ingrained culture of whatever institution
was supposedly being changed, the folks increasingly saw the depravity of the so-called chiefs,
the overlords that controlled goings on in their world, the demons, for that was what the folks also
termed them, that thrived on negativity, they saw through them they saw through their anxieties, their woes.

Yes, the folks realized how much their overlords were anxious about being exposed for what they were
O yes, what they really were, cowards and bullies that wickedly exploited to the brim, entrenched
societal institutions to oppress everyone, more so, those persons they considered their
foes for daring to not 'obey' their lunatic commands, their agendas meant to continue to
degrade the void, at all costs, for that was how they could feed the snake, the ouroboros they had to
keep alive to stay alive and perpetuate their agendas, so, the folks were also very
curious about why their overlords did not like being exposed, for what that meant was verily
mysterious to them, after all, they were wave fields, like every mattered entity, or what the
folks called consciousnesses that manifest as reality in void, waves that became mattered yes
measured, or better put, seen by another mattered entity, perhaps, the folks felt, the concern, yes.

Again, the folks realized they might have struck another key issue, that of their overlords being scared

to death of being seen, verily, measured, so, mattered in the manner the void shared was, the 'brick and
mortar' manner wherein they lived, the folks reckoned these entities did not want to be seen as snakes,
as popping pumpkins, as sticks, as shimmering amorphous whatever, as little green people, or
as mammy water, or whatever else their forms were, the folks started to wonder if this did not
in fact explain the brutality of these entities towards the 'rebels' that attempted to
investigate and expose them, being measured perhaps exposing these cowards to someone punching
their noses or wringing their necks, or seeing them sneak into the loo to recharge their batteries,
like junkies, situations that would not augur well for their claim to some mysterious sinew,
the folks were forging ahead unfazed, they were getting closer to regaining their freedom, O yes.

Things were moving fast, their ranks were swelling exponentially, and they were gaining increasing
confidence in their ability to achieve their goal, so, they forged ahead, they sought even more
information to better understand their so-called overlords, whose so-called alliances of
consciousnesses they were starting to see as vulnerable, as no more than a bunch of crazy
like-minded demented demonic maniacs, which alarmed them, in other words, that the peoples
were under the control of maniacs was alarming to the folks, and made them even more set,
more determined to chase these maniacs out of town, so, they got to work with even more zest, they
worked harder at persuading their folks to jettison the grand narratives of demonic beings
nasty entities, parasites marauding void, destroying their way of life infesting them with bugs killing them in
hundreds of thousands at will the folks and their friends were hellbent on entrenching peace and joy in void.

Book 10

The endgame seemed to be clear to the peoples, the aim of their overlords was to feed the beast: the more they thought about it, the more convinced they were, they also believed their controllers were determined to achieve this goal in cognito, as unidentifiable as possible,
why they could be quite pieced off by anyone that tried to expose them, so, the folks knew yes they were getting closer to achieving their goal of being free, they knew they could achieve their goals exposing their overlords, yes, stripping them naked in the market place, as some of them said, some others, while agreeing that the entities responsible for the troubles not only in the city in
the sun, but also all over the void, needed to be exposed, did not consider it at all
necessary to humiliate them, even as they knew these evil entities were quite mean,
and would not hesitate to humiliate if they could, if not even kill them for being rebels.

They realized their overlords were doing worse things to them, yet the folks all agreed that their faith and their belief in righteousness and in doing only good deeds precluded them for being vengeful and from being vindictive, that they were only interested in peace and in being free, and not in revenge, they said, forging ahead with their inquiries into the nature of their oppressors and in what to do to free themselves from the cycle of oppression in an ouroboros laid, one next question they agreed they needed to ask being who or what did not want to be 'measured' which, in quantum mechanics parlance translated to being mattered, being seen, which made all the folks even more curious about who or what did not want to be punched in the nose, exposed, as some of the folks joked, they needed to know, and why they did not want to be exposed, all jokes apart, they felt it was necessary for them to know who or what was hiding in the crypts, messing with their pates, O yes.

The folks saw these 'shy' entities were wave-fields that could be mattered, so, they were all probably yes, intergalactic entities rather than inter dimensional entities, which meant that they
were all constituents of the energy-exchange transaction-based alliances that indeed constituted the consciousnesses manifesting in the realities they shared, yes, their void, constituents hierarchically placed to express themselves in a gradation of dominance, the most dominant, manifesting the most hegemony and, as such yea, the need for the most secrecy, understandably, the folks figured, with so much energy, in their control, at stake, the need to hide and operate behind the scenes most urgent and important in this cabal than in the lesser 'mortals' constituting the alliances, pretty much, the folks reckoned like the style of the 'invisible' money men and women in void, whose names and faces did not exist!

Yes, the folks agreed, their 'shy' overlords reminded them of these very rich people, or yes, whatever, the wealthiest and most powerful in society were unknown to the public not to mention their identities, what they looked like, whether they were black or white, blue or green, or even red, yet they controlled the so-called leaders, the 'most powerful' this or that in world blabbing all over the place, trysting with fascists socialists and capitalists, with whoever or yes whatever was the highest bidder in their funny energy games: the folks were thrilled, knowing they were on the right track and were getting somewhere with their inquiries, realizing that they were getting closer to the wisdom of a bird, an ibis yea instructive as they forged ahead teasing out complex stuff, figuring out the nitty gritty of a mysterious void, hoping to liberate a city in the sun, and restore peace in paradise, very soon, they all pledged.

They all declared it was a task that must be done, and they were confident they would achieve their goal, they continued to investigate who or what their hidden overlords were and why they were so 'shy' they would kill anyone that dared to investigate them, let alone expose them. Something that crossed their minds in relation to the first question was the sundry forms their bosses might take measured, that is, mattered, perhaps concerned about how the composite mattered, O yes, the predominant atavistic epigenetic epiphenomena termed humans would react to see some bizarre-looking pumpkins popping in and out of space, little green men and women walking down the street holding hands, or necking in the park, the peoples thought the components of the alliances in control in void might be vectored sticks, mattered, or shimmering amorphousness, they imagined they could be viper-headed humanoids or even bipedal ants, forms that might alarm the composite.

It crossed the minds of the folks that the answer to the second question of why their overlords were being discrete was related to the first, albeit perhaps not entirely so, they agreed that it would, probably, be un-strategic for them to be roaming around the city, 'naked,' as bipedal ants, or ambulatory amorphousness, when they could simply stealthily O yes, operate in the composite called the human body, if even with funny eyes, but the folks were all agreed that there was probably more to the story, yes, an aspect of the matter that took them straight to the beast, as they all referred to the super-intelligent or, as some of the folks preferred to say, super-retarded internalized, that is to say, the not matter-able, inter dimensional entities that controlled their overlords, verily, the externalized intergalactic entities that lorded it over the peoples in a void, made life a chore.

So, they were finally where they figured everything started and ended, with Leviathan of the realms, the inter dimensional composite that some referred to as the beast, the destroyer of goodness that the internalized inter dimensional entities of goodness confronted in the paradise wars, the folks began to have a deeper understanding of what was going on in void, why the 'hidden hands' that controlled the ones that ruled over the peoples could not be revealed, why it was immeasurable hence could not be mattered, why the consciousnesses that in void yes 'represented' it had to protect that secret, and not necessarily the beast, yes with unimaginable vigor, and punished those that strayed, either away from their vow having signed up with the devil, or beast to protect the secret, or into the protected zone to probe the nature of the beast or any such thing, yea with equally venomous rage, yes, without a doubt.

Indeed, this conclusion by the folks was very instructive regarding their own observations in void, for example how grand narratives seemed to have such un-understandable strangleholds on their folks how it appeared that all these folks had all been de-humanized and were all nothing more than zombies that 'only' echoed what they appeared to be programmed to say, how it appeared hopeless to persuade them to even klieg their so-called faith in whatever credo or dogma they believed in, how these folks could kill even persons in their folds, 'rebels,' as they might call them, that held even a minimally different doctrinal or ideological view, how all these folks had even what some of their leaders referred to as 'herd mentality,' what some others termed 'group think,' how these persons, as such, still got trashed no matter what they did to please the beast, how these folks appeared trapped in a vicious spider's web for aye, clinging to lies and chicanery they believed.

The peoples were clearly saddened by what they found, which made them decide to redouble their efforts to help therein their kin, and to hope yes to persuade them to revisit their very potent

attachments to their credos dogmas ideologies that simply were concocted to keep them
down as slaves, as the study the peoples continued to carry out showed, so, they kept working very
steadfastly to let their peoples know there was a chance they might be able to retake their city
in the sun from the baleful entities that ruled their precious void, controlled their minds, yes, looked at from
a different angle, or what their consciousnesses manifested gleaned from yet another point
of view, they kept trying to let them know that all was not lost no matter how formidable their
foe was, and reminded them that they did it before and gain control over their lives again, and
that, together, they could seek a better brighter future for their void, a more perfect union forge.

It was clear the peoples were not trying to destroy anyone's faith but to strengthen it, yes, not
along the path of evilness but along the path of goodness, they reminded their folks that they
were builders, not destroyers, that they sought the good of all, not the extinction of the void, noting
that the void was moribund it appeared: they reminded their folks that its rot was, in someway or
another inevitable, many would contend, given the direction the emissaries
of the beast that controlled the void had taken a city in the sun and continued to take it
and the rest of the void, affirming that it was not too late to be on the side of goodness living
virtuously doing good deeds, treading the path of righteousness, which would lead them on the path of
perfection that was the way to turn imperfection to perfection to enable egress from
the belly of a snake to entry into peace in paradise, for life; aye, aye, aye, said them all.